The World Around Me

Poems by Debbie Croft

AF604899

Contents

Colours

The world has lots of colours –
I would like to have them all.
The reds and blues and yellows,
To make pictures for my wall!

Red

The world has lots of colours,
But red is best of all.
The light that stops the cars and trucks,
And apples big and small.

Blue

The world has lots of colours,
But the best of all is blue.
The sky way up above us,
And the sea we swim in, too.

Yellow

The world has lots of colours,
But yellow is the best.
The sun so high up in the sky,
And ducklings in their nest.

Summer

The summer days are long and hot,
But we have lots of fun.
We dive into the swimming pool.
We don't play in the sun!

Autumn Leaves

I love the autumn leaves,
With colours orange, brown and red.
It's fun to sit outside,
And let them fall down on my head.

My Snowman

On Saturday, I made a snowman,
Tall and fat and round.
On Sunday, I went back,
And saw a puddle on the ground!

Spring

In spring, the leaves are green again,
And birds sing in the trees.
There are butterflies with spotted wings,
And lots of buzzing bees.

My Shadow

My shadow likes to play with me.
We walk and skip and run.
She always stays beside me,
When we play out in the sun.

My shadow follows me about,
When I play on the slide.
She comes along the path with me,
When I go for a ride!

When I'm playing football,
She is always there with me.
She kicks the ball just like I do.
It's so much fun to see!

But when the day is over,
Or the clouds block out the sun,
My shadow runs away and hides –
Our play time now is done.

My Eyes

I can see with my two eyes.
My eyes are big and blue.
I look around and see my friends,
And pets and flowers, too.

My Ears

I can hear with my two ears.
My ears hear lots of noise.
I hear the cars and trucks go by,
And songs by girls and boys.

Me

I have a nose, I have a mouth,
I see you have them too.
And **you** have eyes and ears as well,
But I don’t look like you!